For Jose Luis
and Kazia

Copyright © 1988 by Jon Agee
All rights reserved
Library of Congress catalog card number: 87-046072
Published simultaneously in Canada by Collins Publishers, Toronto
Color separations by Photolitho AG., Gossau/Zurich
Printed and bound in the United States of America
by Horowitz/Rae Book Manufacturers
Typography by Constance Fogler
First edition, 1988

THE
INCREDIBLE PAINTING
OF FELIX CLOUSSEAU
JON AGEE

Farrar, Straus & Giroux · New York

IN PARIS, the Royal Palace
was holding its Grand Contest of Art.
From all over the city, painters
came to show their pictures.

One of them was an unknown painter named Felix Clousseau.

All the great artists were there. Gaston du Stroganoff showed *The King on His Throne*. Felicien CaffayOllay showed *The King on Horseback*. Alphonse LeCamembair showed *The King in Armor*.

Then Clousseau showed
his painting.
"Outrageous!" the judges cried.
Never had they seen such
a ridiculous painting.
Then, suddenly—

a sound came from the painting.
The judges were stunned.

Clousseau was awarded the Grand Prize.
They called him a genius.
It was the first time in history
a painting had quacked.

But that was only
half of it.

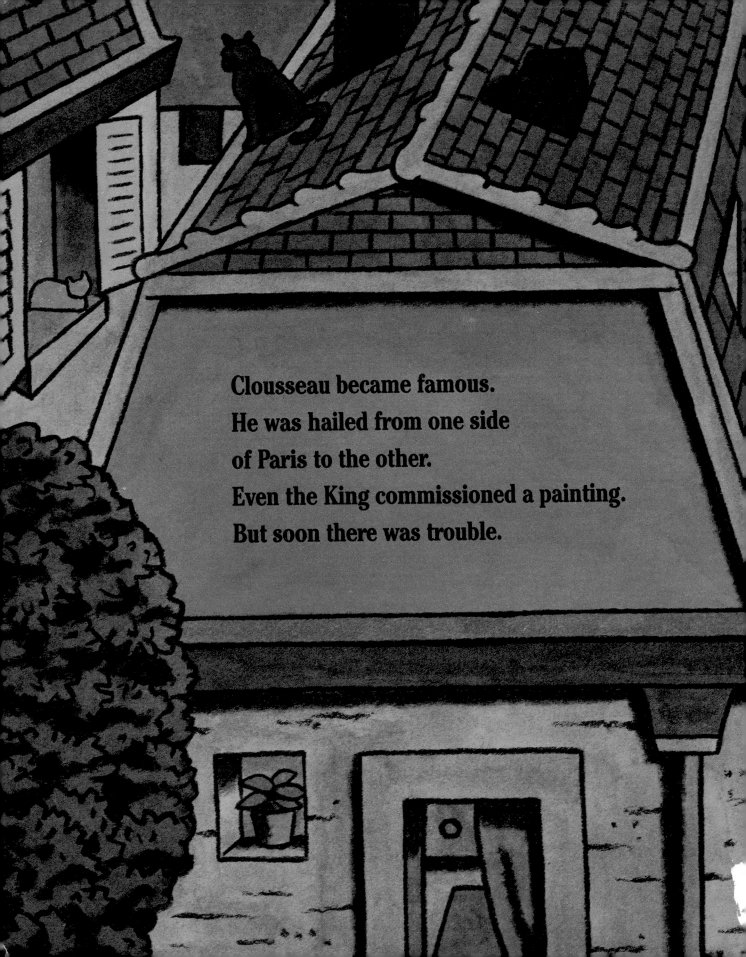

Clousseau became famous.
He was hailed from one side
of Paris to the other.
Even the King commissioned a painting.
But soon there was trouble.

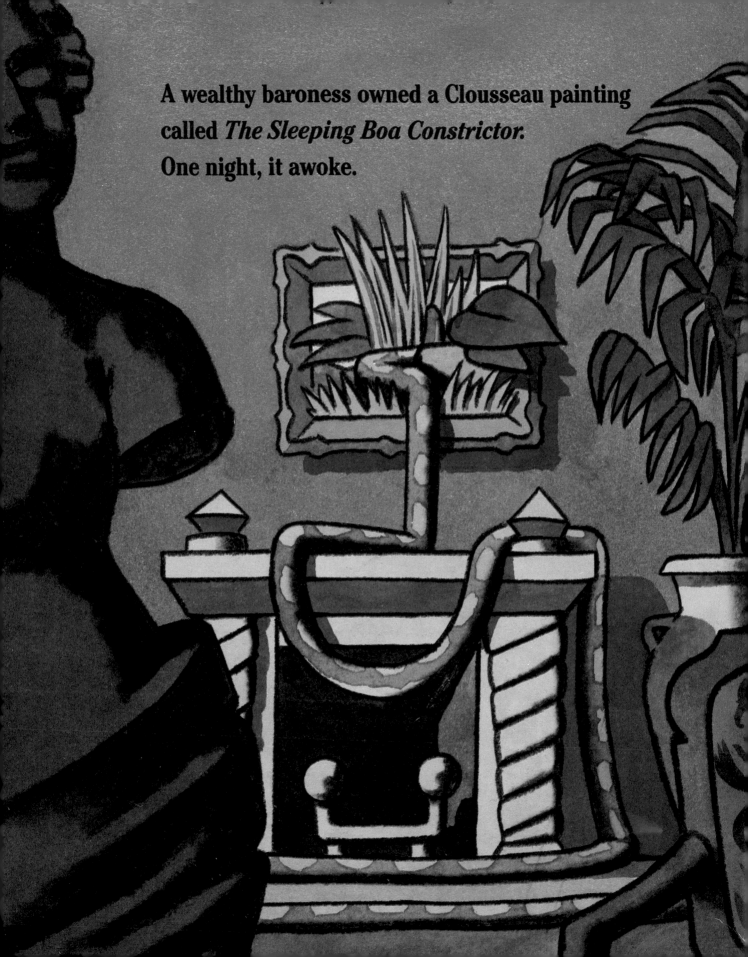

A wealthy baroness owned a Clousseau painting called *The Sleeping Boa Constrictor.* One night, it awoke.

In fact, wherever there was
a Clousseau canvas, there was chaos.

The public was furious!

There were damages! Somebody had to pay!

So Clousseau was sent to prison.

Clousseau's paintings were seized
…all except one.

Meanwhile,
a notorious jewel thief
was on the loose. All over Paris,
diamonds, emeralds, and sapphires
were missing.

One night, the thief
broke into the King's Palace
to steal the crown.

The next morning,
to the King's surprise, he found the thief—
caught in the grasp of a ferocious dog.
The crown was saved.

Clousseau was a hero.

He was awarded the Medal of Honor.

Released from prison,

he went back to his studio...

and returned to his painting.